Clouds

A Modern Translation

Adapted for the Contemporary Reader

Aristophanes

Translated by Tim Zengerink

Table of Contents

Preface - Message to the Reader

What If You Could Help Rebuild the Greatest Library in Human History?

Thousands of years ago, the Library of Alexandria stood as the crown jewel of human achievement — a sanctuary where the collected wisdom of every known civilization was gathered, preserved, and shared freely.

And then, it was lost.

Through fire, conquest, and the slow erosion of time, humanity lost not just books — but ideas, dreams, discoveries, and stories that could have changed the world forever.

Today, the Library of Alexandria lives again — and you are invited to be a part of its restoration.

Our mission is simple yet profound:

To rebuild the greatest library the world has ever known, and to translate all timeless works into every language and dialect, so that no seeker of knowledge is ever left behind again.

By joining our movement to rebuild the modern Library of Alexandria, you become part of an unprecedented mission:

- **Unlimited Access to the Greatest Audiobooks & eBooks Ever Written:**

  Instantly explore thousands of legendary works—Plato, Shakespeare, Jane Austen, Leo Tolstoy, and countless more. All instantly available to read or listen, placing a complete literary universe at your fingertips.

- **Beautiful Paperback & Deluxe Editions at Printing Cost**

  Own any title as an elegant paperback, deluxe hardcover, or stunning collectible boxset—offered to you at true printing cost, delivered straight to your door. Build your personal Library of Alexandria, crafted for beauty, built for durability, and worthy of proud display.

- **Fresh Translations for Modern Readers—in Every Language & Dialect**

  Enjoy timeless masterpieces reimagined in clear, contemporary language—no more outdated phrases or obscure references. Alongside the original versions, we're tirelessly translating these classics into every language and dialect imaginable, ensuring accessibility and understanding across cultures and generations.

- **Join a Global Renaissance of Literature & Knowledge**

  You directly support expanding our library, publishing deluxe editions at true cost, translating works into all global languages, and bringing humanity's greatest stories to people everywhere. By joining today, you're not just preserving a legacy of masterpieces; you set in motion a powerful wave of literary accessibility.

Become a Torchbearer of Knowledge.

Join us for free now at **LibraryofAlexandria.com**

Together, we will ensure that the light of human wisdom never fades again.

With gratitude and a shared love of knowledge,

The Modern Library of Alexandria Team

Visit:

www.libraryofalexandria.com

Or scan the code below:

Introduction:
The Complete Socrates Collection

The Historical Socrates:
The Man, the Martyr, and the Mystery

Socrates stands at the very origin of Western philosophy—an enigmatic figure who wrote nothing, claimed to know nothing, and yet changed everything. Born around 469 BCE in Athens, Socrates lived through a golden yet turbulent period in Greek history, witnessing the rise and fall of the Athenian empire, the Peloponnesian War, the collapse of democratic institutions, and the cultural transition from archaic traditions to rational inquiry. He did not pen treatises or compile systems, but he walked the streets of Athens engaging anyone willing to enter a conversation about virtue, justice, the soul, and the good life. His method was one of questioning, not preaching. His purpose was not to teach doctrine but to awaken thought.

Though he left behind no writings of his own, the legacy of Socrates has been preserved through the works of his students and contemporaries—most famously Plato, Xenophon, and Aristophanes. Each offers a different lens: Plato presents a philosophical dramatization of Socratic dialogue, transforming his teacher into a mouthpiece for the search for eternal truths; Xenophon provides a more pragmatic and moralistic portrait, presenting Socrates as a model citizen and ethical guide; Aristophanes satirizes him as an otherworldly sophist and corrupter of youth in the comedic play The Clouds. Together, these accounts compose a complex mosaic—a "complete Socrates" not as a single historical figure, but as a symbol of philosophy itself: fearless, subversive, inquisitive, and uncompromising in the pursuit of truth.

This collection gathers every major extant account of Socrates across genres and centuries, from the Platonic dialogues and Xenophontic memoirs to the poetic invectives of Aristophanes and scattered references in later philosophical and rhetorical texts. While the texts vary in style, purpose, and tone, they all center on a single figure who has become an archetype of intellectual courage and moral integrity.

Socrates did not build a school or seek wealth. He challenged the powerful, humbled the learned, and insisted that the unexamined life is not worth living. His death—executed by the Athenian state for allegedly corrupting the youth and disrespecting the gods—became the ultimate philosophical gesture. He drank the hemlock not as a defeat, but as a final lesson: that the love of wisdom requires the willingness to suffer, to question, and to die for the truth.

The "Socratic problem"—the challenge of distinguishing the historical Socrates from the literary and philosophical Socrates—is part of the enduring intrigue of his figure. Yet it is precisely this ambiguity that allows Socrates to speak to so many different times and minds. In antiquity, he was a martyr of reason; in the Middle Ages, a pagan prophet; in the Enlightenment, a defender of free inquiry; and in the modern age, a moral iconoclast and philosophical gadfly. In every age, Socrates resurfaces—sometimes as a hero, sometimes as a warning, always as a provocation.

To encounter the complete Socrates is to engage with a life lived in perpetual questioning. He is the philosopher as citizen, the citizen as dissenter, the dissenter as teacher. He offers no final answers, but he offers a path—one walked not through systems but through dialogue, not through authority but through inquiry.

The Dialogues and Portraits: Plato, Xenophon, and Aristophanes

The heart of this collection lies in the dialogues of Plato, where Socrates appears not only as a speaker but as the central moral and philosophical force. Plato's early dialogues—Euthyphro, Apology, Crito, and Phaedo—offer the most direct and poignant image of the Socratic life. In Euthyphro, Socrates questions the nature of piety. In Apology, he defends his life and method before the Athenian jury. In Crito, he refuses escape from prison on principle. And in Phaedo, he dies serenely, discoursing on the immortality of the soul. These four dialogues form a philosophical narrative arc from accusation to execution and remain among the most moving and influential works in all of philosophy.

Beyond these core texts, Socrates continues to feature in Plato's middle and later dialogues—sometimes still as a questioner, sometimes as a symbol of philosophical elevation. In works like Meno, Gorgias, and Protagoras, Socrates challenges the leading intellectuals of the day, exposing the emptiness of their rhetoric and the contradictions in their claims. In Symposium and Phaedrus, he reflects on love, beauty, and divine madness, revealing a more spiritual and mystical dimension. In Republic, he constructs an entire vision of the just society and the tripartite soul. While later dialogues may contain more of Plato than Socrates, they preserve the dramatic spirit of Socratic inquiry—restless, searching, and dialectical.

Xenophon, another student of Socrates, offers a very different portrait. His Memorabilia, Apology, and Symposium present a more conventional and even conservative Socrates—one concerned with daily ethics, self-discipline, and practical virtue. Xenophon's Socrates is a wise, pious, and politically loyal figure, less focused on metaphysical speculation than on the art of living well. While often overshadowed by Plato's more dramatic dialogues, Xenophon's works provide crucial historical insight and preserve aspects of Socratic teaching that Plato may have downplayed or reframed.

Aristophanes, the comic playwright, presents yet another version. In The Clouds, written decades before Socrates' trial, he lampoons Socrates as a head-in-the-clouds intellectual running a "Thinkery" that teaches young men to make the weaker argument appear stronger. This caricature, while exaggerated and humorous, reflects public suspicions about philosophers in democratic Athens—suspicions that would later fuel Socrates' condemnation. Aristophanes' satire is not philosophy, but it is indispensable for understanding the cultural and political reception of Socrates in his own time.

This collection also includes fragments, testimonies, and interpretations from later thinkers—Antisthenes, Aeschines, Cicero, Diogenes Laërtius, and others—who continued to shape the image and memory of Socrates across generations. These varied accounts enrich our understanding of the man and his impact, revealing how different schools—Stoics, Cynics, Neoplatonists—each laid claim to his legacy.

Taken together, these texts present not a single Socrates, but many: the martyr of Athens, the ethical teacher, the cosmological inquirer, the spiritual guide, the political rebel, the literary symbol. The diversity is not a weakness, but a strength. It shows that Socrates cannot be confined to any one role or school—he is philosophy itself, incarnate.

Socratic Philosophy as a Way of Life

More than any other figure, Socrates exemplifies philosophy as a way of life. He did not offer doctrines or dogmas but lived his philosophy in the marketplace, the home, the court, and ultimately the prison. His mission, as he described it in Plato's Apology, was to act as a divine midwife—helping others give birth to ideas, test their beliefs, and live examined lives. He never claimed to have wisdom, only to seek it. And it was this relentless seeking, this refusal to settle for unchallenged assumptions, that became the essence of the philosophical spirit.

At the core of Socratic philosophy lies the belief that the soul—the inner self of reason, conscience, and character—is more important than wealth, status, or even life itself. Socrates taught that to care for one's soul through constant questioning, self-discipline, and pursuit of virtue was the highest human task. He was not concerned with success in the eyes of the world, but with integrity before the truth. He valued the harmony of the soul over the convenience of comfort or the fear of death.

Socratic dialogue is not mere argument; it is a form of spiritual exercise. It breaks down false confidence, exposes contradictions, and forces the interlocutor to confront what they do not know. This process, often painful, is meant to purify the mind and elevate the soul. It requires humility, patience, courage—and above all, love for the truth.

Socrates also redefined the nature of power. For him, true power is not dominance over others, but mastery of the self. The tyrant who cannot control his desires is more enslaved than the prisoner who governs his passions. In this inversion of values, Socrates laid the groundwork for an entirely new conception of ethics—one based on inner excellence rather than external success.

His death, far from extinguishing his influence, immortalized it. By choosing to die rather than abandon his principles, Socrates showed that philosophy is not a luxury or abstraction but a moral necessity. He became a symbol of integrity, a witness to the possibility of a life devoted to truth, and a martyr to the cause of free thought.

In this collection, readers will find the full spectrum of Socratic life and thought—his questions, his silences, his ironies, his convictions. They will witness the birth of philosophy not in the academy, but in conversation; not in doctrines, but in dialogue. They will come to see that the legacy of Socrates is not just a set of texts, but a call to action: to question, to reflect, to live with intention.

The Complete Socrates Collection is more than a compilation—it is an invitation to transformation. It reminds us that wisdom is not given, but pursued; that knowledge is not static, but dynamic; that the examined life is the path not only to understanding, but to meaning. Whether you are new to philosophy or returning to its roots, this collection offers an unparalleled journey through the mind and spirit of one of history's most profound thinkers. Let the dialogues begin— and may they never end.

Foreword

Socrates on Stage: Comedy, Criticism, and the Public Image of Philosophy

Aristophanes' Clouds is one of the most influential and controversial portrayals of Socrates in all of classical literature. Premiered in 423 BCE at the City Dionysia festival in Athens, this comedic play famously satirizes the figure of Socrates as the head of a ludicrous "Thinkery"—a school where students are taught to defy traditional morality, twist arguments, and reject the gods of the city. Far from the austere philosopher of Plato's dialogues or the moral guide of Xenophon's writings, Aristophanes' Socrates is a floating, ridiculous sophist who trains impressionable youths to make the weaker argument defeat the stronger. This caricature had immense cultural impact, and according to Plato's Apology, even Socrates himself blamed Clouds for contributing to the prejudice that led to his trial and execution.

Despite its comedic exaggeration and philosophical distortion, Clouds remains an essential text in the Complete Socrates Collection. It represents how Socrates was perceived (or misperceived) by some segments of Athenian society. More importantly, it serves as a cultural mirror, revealing the social tensions of the time: between old and new generations, between tradition and intellectual innovation, and between the values of the polis and the emergent power of rational discourse. In placing Socrates onstage, Aristophanes transforms him into a symbol of everything Athens found threatening about the new intellectuals—mocking, unorthodox, clever, and subversive.

Yet Clouds is more than just a comedic attack. It is also a serious play in disguise. Beneath the farce lies a rich exploration of language, education, moral relativism, and the fragile foundations of civic authority. In this sense, Aristophanes is not merely targeting Socrates, but raising profound questions about the cost of intellectual freedom and the limits of traditional piety. The play may distort Socrates' philosophy, but it captures with piercing insight the cultural anxiety that surrounded his life and teachings. That makes it not only a historical artifact but a necessary part of any honest reckoning with Socrates' legacy.

The Comic Socrates: Sophistry, Subversion, and Athenian Anxiety

In Clouds, the main character is not Socrates himself, but Strepsiades—an aging, debt-ridden farmer desperate to escape the obligations created by his spoiled, horse-obsessed son, Pheidippides. Believing that the only way out is to learn how to win arguments unjustly, Strepsiades enrolls in the Thinkery run by Socrates, where he hopes to gain the rhetorical tools to cheat his creditors in court. Socrates is introduced suspended in a basket, literally above the world, contemplating the heavens and communicating with clouds, who serve as the chorus and are venerated as the new deities of intellectual enlightenment.

This portrayal is comic and absurd, but it reflects a deep-seated anxiety about the destabilizing effects of sophistry and intellectual skepticism. Socrates, though never historically a sophist, is lumped in with the intellectuals who taught rhetoric for money and were seen as corruptors of traditional Athenian values. In the play, Socrates teaches about clouds, insects, and obscure theories of natural causation, all the while undermining belief in Zeus and traditional gods. He introduces Strepsiades to two personified arguments: the Superior (Just) and Inferior (Unjust) Logoi, who debate the merits of old-fashioned virtue versus newfangled cleverness.

The comedic brilliance of Aristophanes lies in how he uses farce to articulate serious cultural tensions. By presenting Socrates as a figure who literally elevates himself above the city and teaches nonsense in the name of wisdom, Aristophanes taps into fears about the fragmentation of Athenian identity. The move from oral tradition to rational critique, from civic myth to private speculation, was felt by many as a kind of betrayal—a turning away from the communal and religious foundations of the city.

Yet the play is not simply reactionary. Aristophanes is too sophisticated to offer a simple defense of tradition. His critique is more complex: he acknowledges the appeal of intellectual inquiry, the shortcomings of old morality, and the dangers of an unthinking public. What Clouds ultimately dramatizes is the cultural disorientation caused by the rise of the philosophical life. It asks: What happens when reason is untethered from virtue? What happens when education ceases to aim at the good, and instead becomes a tool for manipulation?

In the final act, Strepsiades uses his newfound skills to justify his son beating him—an allegory for the erosion of traditional authority. When he realizes he has been deceived and corrupted, he burns down the Thinkery, denouncing Socrates and his methods. The audience is left with an ambiguous lesson: neither blind adherence to tradition nor unexamined intellectualism seems adequate. The play ends in ashes, not because philosophy is wrong, but because Athens has failed to integrate it properly.

Why Clouds Belongs in the Complete Socrates

Collection

While Clouds is not a philosophical dialogue, and while its Socrates bears little resemblance to the careful moral inquirer of Plato or Xenophon, the play is indispensable to understanding the full legacy of Socrates. It shows us not what Socrates thought, but what he was thought to be—how the popular imagination saw him, and how comedy could both distort and reveal cultural truths.

First, Clouds helps explain the political and social climate that led to Socrates' trial. Plato's Apology directly references Aristophanes' influence, suggesting that the caricature of Socrates as an atheist and corrupter had deep roots in public perception. This portrayal likely shaped the jury's assumptions more powerfully than any single philosophical argument. In this sense, Clouds is part of the trial before the trial—an informal public indictment dressed in satire.

Second, Aristophanes' play forces us to confront the gap between philosophical intention and public reception. Socrates may have seen himself as a moral midwife, but to some Athenians he appeared as a social threat. Clouds explores this disconnect, raising questions about how philosophy should relate to society. Is the philosopher responsible for how his teachings are misused? Can wisdom be dangerous in the wrong hands? These questions remain relevant in any age.

Third, Clouds underscores the need for philosophical literacy. By presenting a world where rhetoric is divorced from ethics, and cleverness from wisdom, Aristophanes warns us of the perils of education without virtue. His critique is not just of Socrates but of a society that cannot distinguish between true philosophy and empty argument. In this way, the play is not anti-intellectual, but anti-cynical—a defense of integrity masked as mockery.

Finally, the inclusion of Clouds in the Complete Socrates Collection affirms that philosophy does not exist in a vacuum. Socrates was not only a thinker but a public figure, and his legacy was shaped by art as well as argument. Aristophanes shows us how philosophy is received, resisted, and reimagined by the culture in which it lives. That perspective is essential for any serious engagement with the Socratic tradition.

In conclusion, Clouds is a masterwork of comic literature and cultural critique. It distorts Socrates to reveal something profound about Athens, philosophy, and the challenge of education. It belongs in the Complete Socrates Collection not because it tells us what Socrates believed, but because it shows us why those beliefs mattered—and why they were feared. To understand Socrates fully, we must understand not only how he spoke, but how he was seen. And no work captures that vision with more wit, ambiguity, or brilliance than Clouds by Aristophanes.

Clouds

Characters

Strepsiades

Phidippides

Strepsiades' Servant

Students of Socrates

Socrates

Chorus of Clouds

Right Argument

Wrong Argument

Pasias

Amynias

Witness

Chaerephon

Scene

A bedroom at night. Strepsiades, Phidippides, and two servants are asleep in their beds. A small house is visible in the distance. It's the middle of the night.

Strepsiades (sitting up in bed):

Ugh! This night feels like it's never going to end! Jupiter, why are the nights so long? When will it be morning? I've already heard the rooster crow. Everyone else is snoring away—something they never used to do! Curse this war! I can't even scold my servants properly anymore.

And this spoiled boy over here—he doesn't wake up at all! He's just curled up comfortably in five blankets.

Well, I guess that's the trend now. I might as well wrap up and try to sleep too.

[Lies back down, but quickly sits up again.]

But I can't sleep! I'm a wreck. My mind won't stop racing because of all the money I owe, the horses I keep, and all the debt—thanks to him!

Look at him—long hair, obsessed with riding, racing chariots, and dreaming about horses—while I lie here losing my mind every time the moon shows it's the twentieth of the month and the interest piles up.

Hey, boy! Light a lamp and bring me my account book. I need to see how much I owe and figure out the interest.

[A servant enters with a lamp and a tablet.]

Okay, let's see… What do I owe?

Twelve minae to Pasias.

Twelve?! Why did I borrow that?

Oh right—when I bought that fancy racehorse.

Ugh! I wish someone had thrown a rock at that horse and blinded it before I bought it!

Phidippides (talking in his sleep):

Not fair, Philo! Stay in your own lane!

Strepsiades:

See? This is exactly what's ruined me. Even in his sleep he's talking about racing horses.

Phidippides:

How many laps will the chariots race?

Strepsiades:

You've got me running in circles too, son. Now, what else do I owe?

Three minae to Amynias—for a tiny chariot and some wheels.

Phidippides:

Walk the horse back after a good rubdown.

Strepsiades:

You fool! You've polished me right out of my money! I've lost court cases, and now people are saying I need to offer property as security for all the unpaid interest.

Phidippides (waking up):

Father, why are you so upset? You've been tossing and turning all night.

Strepsiades:

Because debt collectors are crawling into my blankets and biting me!

Phidippides:

Come on, let me sleep a little longer, will you?

Strepsiades:

Fine. Go ahead and sleep. But just know, all these debts will come crashing down on your head soon enough.

[Phidippides rolls over and goes back to sleep.]

Oh no! I wish that matchmaker had never existed—the one who convinced me to marry your mother. I used to love living in the countryside—simple, unshaven, lying around however I liked, surrounded by bees, sheep, and plenty of olive cake. But then I, a country guy, married a niece of Megacles—yes, the same Megacles. She was from the city: proud, spoiled, and totally obsessed with fancy things.

When we got married, I smelled like wine, cheese, and wool. She, on the other hand, smelled like perfume, saffron, fancy kisses, luxury, overeating, and the perfumes of Colias and Genetyllis. I won't say she was lazy—she did weave. I would show her this old cloak and say, "Look, honey, you're doing a great job weaving!"

[The servant enters again.]

Servant: We're out of oil for the lamp.

Strepsiades: Oh great! Why did you light the lamp that drinks oil so fast? Come here—I ought to make you cry!

Servant: Why should I cry?

Strepsiades: Because you used one of the thick wicks!

[The servant runs out.]

After that, we had a son—me and my "wonderful" wife. Of course, we immediately argued over what to name him. She wanted something fancy like Xanthippus, Charippus, or Callipides—something with "hippos" in it. I wanted to name him after his grandfather—Phidonides. We argued for a while, then finally compromised and named him Phidippides.

She would cradle him and say, "When you grow up, you'll drive your chariot into the city like Megacles, wearing a fancy robe." And I would say, "No, when you're older, you'll wear a simple leather tunic and herd goats from the hills, like your dad."

But he didn't listen to me. Instead, he caught the horse-craze and burned through all my money. Now, after thinking all night, I've come up with one perfect plan. If I can just convince this boy to go along with it, I'll be saved.

But first, I need to wake him up gently. Hmm… what's the nicest way to do it?

Phidippides, my little Phidippides?

Phidippides: What is it, Dad?

Strepsiades: Give me a kiss, and your right hand.

Phidippides: Okay, here. What's going on?

Strepsiades: Tell me—do you love me?

Phidippides: Of course, by Equestrian Poseidon!

Strepsiades: No, don't swear by that god! He's the reason I'm in this mess. But if you really love me, son, then do what I ask.

Phidippides: What do you want me to do?

Strepsiades: Change your ways quickly, and go learn what I'm about to suggest.

Phidippides: What is it you want me to learn?

Strepsiades: Will you promise to do it?

Phidippides: By Dionysus, yes, I will.

Strepsiades: Okay, look over there. See that little door and that small house?

Phidippides: I see it. What about it?

Strepsiades: That's a school of deep thinkers. Inside are men who claim the sky is like an oven, and we're just the coals inside. If you pay them, they'll teach you how to win any argument—right or wrong.

Phidippides: Who are these people?

Strepsiades: I'm not sure what they're called exactly. They're clever philosophers, that's for sure.

Phidippides: Ugh, I know who you mean. They're a bunch of fakes—those pale, barefoot weirdos like that awful Socrates and his buddy Chaerephon.

Strepsiades: Stop! Don't talk nonsense. If you care about your father's land and money, join them and forget about horse riding.

Phidippides: No way, by Dionysus! Not even if you gave me all of Leogoras's pheasants!

Strepsiades: Please, son, I'm begging you—go and get taught!

Phidippides: And what exactly am I supposed to learn?

Strepsiades:

They say that in that school, they teach two kinds of arguments—the stronger one, whatever that means, and the weaker one. But they also say that the weaker one wins even if it defends something wrong. So if you learn how to argue like that—using the weaker argument to win—I wouldn't have to pay back any of the debts I owe because of you.

Phidippides:

I can't do that. I wouldn't even be able to face the noble horsemen if I lost all my honor.

Strepsiades:

Then, by Demeter, you won't eat a single bite of my food—neither you nor your fancy racehorse. I'll throw you both out of the house!

Phidippides:

Uncle Megacles won't let me go without a horse. I'm going inside and ignoring you.

[Phidippides exits.]

Strepsiades:

Even if I'm down, I won't give up! I'll pray to the gods and go to that thinking school myself to learn their tricks. But I'm an old man—how am I supposed to understand these complicated ideas?

Still, I have to try. Why am I just standing here? I should knock!

[He knocks on the door.]

Hey, boy! Hello?

Disciple (from inside):

Go away! Who's banging on the door like that?

Strepsiades:

It's Strepsiades, son of Phidon, from Cicynna.

Disciple:

You're a fool, I swear! You kicked the door so hard you made me lose my train of thought!

Strepsiades:

Sorry! I live far out in the country. But tell me—what were you thinking about before I interrupted?

Disciple:

I can't tell you. It's a secret for students only.

Strepsiades:

Well, then tell me anyway—I came here to become a student at this school of thinkers.

Disciple:

Alright, but you have to treat this like a mystery. So, Socrates asked Chaerephon how far a flea could jump—how many times its own foot length. See, it had bitten Chaerephon's eyebrow and jumped onto Socrates' head.

Strepsiades:

And how did he measure that?

Disciple:

Brilliantly. He melted some wax, dipped the flea's feet into it, and let the wax harden into tiny shoes. Then, using those as little slippers, he measured how far the flea jumped.

Strepsiades:

Wow, by Zeus! That's genius!

Disciple:

That's nothing. Want to hear another of Socrates' inventions?

Strepsiades:

Yes, please! I'm begging you!

Disciple:

Chaerephon asked him whether gnats buzz from their mouths or from their behinds.

Strepsiades:

And what did Socrates say?

Disciple:

He said the gnat's guts are very narrow, and the wind rushes through its body to the back end. The rear, being hollow, echoes the air like a trumpet when it rushes through.

Strepsiades:

So a gnat's butt is like a bugle? That's amazing! A guy who knows that much could win any case in court!

Disciple:

But a lizard recently ruined one of his best ideas.

Strepsiades:

How? Tell me!

Disciple:

He was studying the moon's path in the sky—looking straight up with his mouth open—and a lizard dropped on him from the ceiling!

Strepsiades:

A lizard hit Socrates? That's hilarious!

Disciple:

And last night, we had no dinner.

Strepsiades:

So what did he do about food?

Disciple:

He sprinkled ashes on the table, bent a small spit into a compass shape, and used it to sneak a cloak from the gymnasium.

Strepsiades:

And people admire Thales?! Quick—open the door to the thinking school and let me meet Socrates! I want to be a student right now! Hurry—open it!

[The door opens. Inside, Socrates' students are staring down at the ground. Socrates is seen floating in a basket above them.]

Good heavens! What kind of creatures are these?

Disciple:

What surprises you? What do these people remind you of?

Strepsiades:

They look like those Spartan prisoners from the battle of Pylos. But why are they all staring at the ground?

Disciple:

They're looking for things under the earth.

Strepsiades:

So they're hunting for roots? I could help them with that—I know where some big, tasty ones are. But what about those guys bending over like that?

Disciple:

They're searching in the darkness beneath the underworld.

Strepsiades:

Then why are their butts pointing up at the sky?

Disciple:

That's how they study astronomy—through their rear ends!

[Turning to the students.]

Okay, go back inside before he bothers you too much.

Strepsiades:

Wait, not yet! Let them stay. I want to ask them something real quick.

Disciple:

They're not allowed to be out in the open air for too long.

[The students go inside.]

Strepsiades:

Whoa—what's all this stuff? What does it do?

Disciple:

That's astronomy.

Strepsiades:

And what about this?

Disciple:

Geometry.

Strepsiades:

What's that used for?

Disciple:

To measure land.

Strepsiades:

You mean land for farming?

Disciple:

No, the entire earth.

Strepsiades:

Well, that's a smart idea. Sounds useful—and fair to everyone!

Disciple:

(Pointing at a map) Look here. This is a map of the whole world. See that? That's Athens.

Strepsiades:

Are you serious? I don't believe it. I don't see any judges!

Disciple:

I promise you, this is really Athens.

Strepsiades:

Then where are my neighbors from Cicynna?

Disciple:

They're right here. And over here is Euboea, stretched out long beside it.

Strepsiades:

Yeah, I know. We stretched it ourselves—me and Pericles. But where's Sparta?

Disciple:

It's here.

Strepsiades:

So close? You'd better do something to push it farther away!

Disciple:

Sorry, by Zeus—it can't be done.

Strepsiades:

Then you'll regret it!

[He suddenly notices Socrates above.]

Hey—who's that man up in the basket?

Disciple:

That's him.

Strepsiades:

Him who?

Disciple:

Socrates.

Strepsiades:

Oh, Socrates! Please, shout up and call him down for me.

Disciple:

Nope. Call him yourself. I'm busy.

[The Disciple exits.]

Strepsiades:

Socrates! Hey, my little Socrates!

Socrates:

Why are you calling me, mortal creature?

Strepsiades:

Please tell me—what are you doing up there?

Socrates:

I'm walking through the air, thinking about the sun.

Strepsiades:

So you're looking down on the gods from way up in that basket instead of thinking from the ground?

Socrates:

Exactly. I wouldn't be able to understand the sky unless I lifted my mind into the air and blended my thoughts with the atmosphere. If I stayed on the ground and looked up, I'd never figure anything out. The earth pulls thinking downward like it does moisture. Even watercress suffers the same problem.

Strepsiades:

Wait—you're saying thinking draws moisture to watercress? Come down here, little Socrates, and teach me all this stuff. That's why I came!

[Socrates lowers himself and steps out of the basket.]

Socrates:

Alright, why exactly did you come?

Strepsiades:

I want to learn how to argue. I'm drowning in debt from nasty lenders, and they keep seizing my property.

Socrates:

How'd you end up in debt without realizing it?

Strepsiades:

It was a horse addiction—so expensive and so greedy! But teach me that other kind of argument, the one that wins but doesn't pay back anything. I swear by the gods, I'll pay you whatever you ask!

Socrates:

By which gods? We don't really use gods as currency around here.

Strepsiades:

Then what do you swear by? Iron coins like in Byzantium?

Socrates:

Would you like to really understand how the sky works?

Strepsiades:

Yes, by Zeus—if that's even possible!

Socrates:

And do you want to speak with the Clouds, who are our divine powers?

Strepsiades:

Absolutely!

Socrates (very seriously):

Then take a seat on this sacred couch.

Strepsiades:

Alright, I'm sitting!

Socrates:

Then take this wreath and put it on.

Strepsiades:

Why the wreath? Oh no—Socrates, please don't sacrifice me like they did with Athamas!

Socrates:

No, no. This is just part of the ceremony for students who are being initiated.

Strepsiades:

So what am I going to get out of this?

Socrates:

You'll become sharp at arguing—clever, talkative, and able to twist words easily. Now be quiet.

Strepsiades:

By Zeus, I don't believe you! If you sprinkle something on me, I'll turn into flour!

Socrates:

You should be saying positive things and listen carefully to my prayer.

O mighty King Air, who holds the earth up high, and you, bright Aether, and you, majestic goddesses—the Clouds—who send thunder and lightning, rise up now and appear in the sky to this curious student of yours!

Strepsiades:

Wait, wait! Not yet! Let me wrap myself in this cloak so I don't get soaked. I can't believe I left home without a hat—what bad luck!

Socrates:

Come now, Clouds, you honored ones, reveal yourselves to this man.

Whether you're on the snowy peaks of Olympus, or dancing with the sea-nymphs in Father Ocean's garden, or drawing water from the Nile in golden pots, or resting near the frozen lake of Maeotis or the icy cliffs of Mimas—please listen to our prayer, accept our offering, and bless our ceremony.

[Thunder rumbles as the Chorus of Clouds sings from afar.]

Chorus:

We are the eternal Clouds! Let's rise up and look down with our clear and misty forms.

From the deep ocean, up to the tall mountain tops covered in forests,

let's gaze at the watchtowers, the crops, and the sacred earth.

Let's see the rushing rivers and the roaring sea,

as the sky glows with shining light.

Come, let's shake the water from our divine forms

and look over the world with wide, watchful eyes.

Socrates:

O powerful Clouds, you heard me when I called!

[Turning to Strepsiades]

Did you hear their voices—and the thunder? It sounded like a god, didn't it?

Strepsiades:

Yes, I bow to you, great ones. That thunder shook me to my bones. I'm so nervous now I almost—well—I really need to go to the bathroom...

Socrates:

Don't joke around like those silly poets. Say only respectful things. A whole group of goddesses is arriving, singing their sacred songs.

Chorus:

Let's go, rain-bringing sisters, to the rich land of Athens,

to see the beloved home of Cecrops—brave and full of noble people.

There, sacred traditions are kept secret and respected.

There are holy temples, grand statues, and offerings to the gods.

There are festivals all year long,

especially in spring, when the city celebrates Bacchus with music, dancing,

and the sweet sounds of flutes.

Strepsiades:

Socrates, please, tell me—by Zeus—who are those voices singing such a beautiful song? Are they goddesses?

Socrates:

Not exactly. They're the Clouds—divine spirits who help lazy thinkers.

They give us clever ideas, tricky arguments, big words, sneaky tricks, and mental sharpness.

Strepsiades:

Now I understand why I felt a spark inside me when I heard them.

My brain is already itching to argue about tiny things like smoke and to pick apart sayings with clever little points.

I really want to see them now—if that's even possible.

Socrates:

Then look over there, toward Mount Parnes.

I can see them gently floating down.

Strepsiades:

Where? Show me!

Socrates:

Right there—they're coming down in a big group through the valleys and trees, from the side.

Strepsiades:

What are you talking about? I still can't see them.

Socrates:

They're right there—by the entrance.

[The Chorus enters.]

Strepsiades:

Now I finally see them! It took a while.

Socrates:

You see them now for sure—unless your eyes are full of pumpkins!

Strepsiades:

Yes, by Zeus! Oh, how amazing—those Clouds are covering everything!

Socrates:

But didn't you already know they were goddesses?

Strepsiades:

No way! I thought they were just fog, mist, or smoke.

Socrates:

That's because you didn't know better. These goddesses actually support all kinds of thinkers—fortune tellers, healers, lazy guys with long hair and fancy rings, people who write chorus songs, and weather experts. Basically, they help people who don't do real work but who praise them in poetry.

Strepsiades:

So that's why in poems they say things like "the fierce spinning clouds," "Typho's wild winds," "raging storms," and "moist sky-birds floating through the air," and "rain falling from the misty Clouds." And what do these poets get in return? Big, tasty fish and roasted birds!

Socrates:

So isn't it fair that the Clouds reward them?

Strepsiades:

Okay, but tell me this—if these really are Clouds, why do they look like women? That doesn't make sense.

Socrates:

Then what do you think they look like?

Strepsiades:

I don't really know. But if anything, they look more like fluffy wool than women. Clouds don't have noses!

Socrates:

Just answer my question.

Strepsiades:

Go ahead—ask away.

Socrates:

Have you ever looked at the sky and seen a cloud that looked like a centaur, or a panther, or a wolf, or a bull?

Strepsiades:

Of course I have! But what about it?

Socrates:

They can become whatever they want. So if they see someone wild and hairy—like that guy Xenophantes' son—they turn into centaurs to make fun of him.

Strepsiades:

And what if they saw Simon the thief? What would they do?

Socrates:

They'd become wolves—to show what kind of person he is.

Strepsiades:

Ah! That explains why yesterday, when they saw Cleonymus the coward, they turned into deer. They saw how scared he was.

Socrates:

Exactly. And now that they've seen Clisthenes, they look like women.

Strepsiades:

Hail, mighty goddesses! Please—if you've ever spoken to anyone before—speak to me now! Let your voices reach the heavens, great queens!

Chorus:

Greetings, old man, seeker of smart words!

And you, teacher of strange, clever things!

Tell us what you want. We won't listen to just any philosopher—only to wise ones like Prodicus, because he's smart. And we'll speak with you, Socrates, because you walk the streets with confidence, with your eyes cast sideways, barefoot, enduring hardship, and trusting in us. That's why we've come.

Strepsiades:

Oh wow—what a voice! It's so holy and beautiful and powerful!

Socrates:

Yes, they're the only real goddesses. Everything else is nonsense.

Strepsiades:

Wait, wait! Are you telling me that Jupiter—the Olympian—isn't a god?

Socrates:

Jupiter? Don't be silly. There's no such god.

Strepsiades:

What?! Then who makes it rain? Tell me that first!

Socrates:

The Clouds, of course. I can prove it.

Have you ever seen it rain without Clouds? No, right? So if Jupiter made the rain, he should be able to do it in clear skies without them.

Strepsiades:

By Apollo, you've got a point! I used to think Jupiter caused rain. But now tell me—who makes the thunder? That always scares me.

Socrates:

The Clouds again. When they move around, they thunder.

Strepsiades:

How?! Tell me, you bold genius!

Socrates:

When the Clouds get full of water and can't hold it anymore, they crash into each other. That makes a loud boom—that's thunder.

Strepsiades:

But who makes them crash into each other? Isn't that Jupiter?

Socrates:

No, it's the Air—what we call the Vortex.

Strepsiades:

Vortex?! I had no idea Jupiter was out and Vortex was in charge now. But you still haven't explained the actual thunder clap.

Socrates:

I already did! The Clouds bang into each other when they're heavy with water. That makes the thunder sound.

Strepsiades:

Hmm… I'm still not totally convinced.

Socrates:

Then let me explain it using you as an example. Have you ever eaten too much soup during the Panathenaic festival and suddenly had your stomach make a loud rumbling noise?

Strepsiades:

Yes, by Apollo! As soon as I eat a little soup, my stomach starts acting up. First, it rumbles quietly like this—pappax, pappax. Then it gets louder—papa-pappax. And finally, it booms out loud like thunder—papapappax! Just like that!

Socrates:

Now think about it—if your tiny stomach can make that kind of noise, isn't it more likely that the vast sky can thunder even louder?

Strepsiades:

That makes sense! Even the words "trump" and "thunder" sound alike. But tell me this—where does lightning come from? You know, that firebolt that burns things up when it strikes, and scorches those who survive? I've always thought Zeus throws it at people who lie under oath.

Socrates:

Oh, come on! That's such an old-fashioned belief. If Zeus punishes liars, why hasn't he struck down Simon, Cleonymus, or Theorus? Those guys lie all the time! Instead, the lightning hits his own temple, or places like Cape Sunium or big oak trees. Do oak trees lie?

Strepsiades:

You've got a point. I never thought of it that way. So what is lightning then?

Socrates:

It happens when dry wind rises up and gets trapped inside the Clouds. The pressure makes the Cloud puff up like a balloon. Then, when the pressure is too much, the Cloud bursts open, and the air rushes out fast. Because of the speed and friction, it catches fire and becomes lightning.

Strepsiades:

Oh wow, that's exactly what happened to me once at the Diasia festival! I was cooking a sausage for my relatives, and I forgot to poke holes in it. It puffed up, burst open, and burned my face!

Chorus:

Oh mortal who seeks deep wisdom from us!

If you have a strong memory, if you think deeply, if you can endure long hours of standing or walking, if you don't mind the cold, if you're okay skipping meals and staying away from wine and silly sports, then you'll be a clever man. And being clever means winning through words and ideas.

Strepsiades:

Don't worry—I'm tough! I'm used to rough beds and simple food. My stomach doesn't complain. I'm ready for anything you throw at me.

Socrates:

Then, are you ready to stop believing in any gods except for Chaos, the Clouds, and the Tongue?

Strepsiades:

Absolutely! I won't even talk to the others if I see them. No more sacrifices, prayers, or incense.

Chorus:

Tell us what you want. Ask boldly. If you admire us and want to be smart, you'll get what you ask for.

Strepsiades:

Great mistresses, all I ask is this one small thing: I want to be the best speaker in all of Greece—by a hundred stadium lengths!

Chorus:

You've got it! From now on, no one will get more votes than you in the Assembly.

Strepsiades:

I'm not trying to make big speeches or change the world. I just want to twist the truth, avoid paying my debts, and win in court!

Chorus:

Then that's exactly what you'll get. Your request is modest. Put yourself in our helpers' hands.

Strepsiades:

I trust you. I've got no choice! Horses and marriage ruined me. So do what you must. I give you my body—to go hungry, thirsty, cold, dirty, beaten—whatever it takes. If it gets me out of debt and makes me sound smart and bold, I'm in! I'll lie, argue, twist the truth, talk in circles—anything! People can call me a trickster, a liar, a weasel, a crook, a loudmouth, a smooth-talker, a fraud, or a street hustler—fine by me. Let them even turn me into a sausage and serve me to the deep thinkers if they want!

Chorus:

This guy is brave and determined! If you learn from us, you'll be as famous as the stars.

Strepsiades:

What kind of life will I have?

Chorus:

The best one a mortal could live. People will line up at your door just to talk with you. They'll ask your advice about lawsuits and big cases. You'll be known everywhere for your sharp mind.

[To Socrates:]

Go ahead—start teaching him slowly. Test his brain and see what he's ready for.

Socrates:

Alright, tell me a bit about how your mind works. Once I know that, I'll know what tools to use to teach you.

Strepsiades:

Wait—are you planning to lay siege to my brain?

Socrates:

No, no. I just want to know if you have a good memory.

Strepsiades:

Well, it depends! If someone owes me money, I remember perfectly. But if I owe someone else, I forget everything!

Socrates:

Hmm. Do you think you were born with the natural gift of speaking well?

Strepsiades:

I'm not really good at talking—but I'm great at cheating.

Socrates:

Then how will you ever learn?

Strepsiades:

I'll learn just fine. Don't worry.

Socrates:

Alright then. But you need to make sure that when I say something deep and tricky, you catch it right away.

Strepsiades:

So what—you want me to snap up wisdom like a dog chasing snacks?

Socrates:

You're hopeless... I can already tell, old man, you're going to need a few beatings. Let me ask—what do you usually do when someone hits you?

Strepsiades:

I take it for a bit, then I get some witnesses, and soon after, I sue them.

Socrates:

Alright then, take off your cloak.

Strepsiades:

Did I do something wrong?

Socrates:

No, it's just our rule—everyone enters without a cloak.

Strepsiades:

What? I'm not here to search for stolen stuff!

Socrates:

Just take it off. Stop being ridiculous.

Strepsiades:

Okay, but if I really try and work hard, which one of your students will I be like?

Socrates:

You'll be just like Chaerephon in intelligence.

Strepsiades:

Oh no! That guy's half-dead!

Socrates:

Stop talking and follow me quickly.

Strepsiades:

At least give me a honey cake to calm my nerves. I feel like I'm about to enter a spooky cave.

Socrates:

Come on—why are you dawdling at the door?

[Socrates and Strepsiades go inside.]

Chorus:

Go in peace, brave man. May good luck follow you for seeking knowledge, even in your old age. You're doing something amazing—learning new things and sharpening your mind!

[Turning to the audience:]

Dear audience, I'm going to be honest with you. By Dionysus, the god who raised me—I truly believe you are smart people, and this is the smartest of my plays. I put everything I had into it. But last time I brought it to the festival, some foolish people gave the prize to a less worthy comedy. That hurt, especially because I wrote this play for an audience like you—intelligent, thoughtful people.

Still, I won't give up on you. Ever since my earlier plays, like The Modest Man and The Rake, won your approval, I've felt your support. Back then, I was just starting out—I hadn't even written much—and you helped raise my work like your own child. You've always backed me.

This play is like Electra, coming to find its long-lost brother in the crowd. You'll know it when you see it—if you're the smart audience I believe you are.

She's modest too—no rude costumes or cheap laughs. No fake body parts to get kids giggling, no mocking bald guys, no slapstick comedy. She's not rushing around with torches yelling nonsense. She's come quietly, confident in her own words.

And me? I don't recycle old material over and over like some lazy poets. I always bring you something new and clever. Remember how I dared to mock Cleon when he was powerful—and I didn't kick him when he was down. But now every hack playwright keeps mocking poor Hyperbolus. They copy my jokes—like the one about eels—and pretend it's theirs. Eupolis even stole from my play The Knights, added a drunk old lady just for laughs, and called it Maricas. Total rip-off.

Then Hermippus made fun of Hyperbolus, and now everyone else piles on. If you laugh at them, don't expect to enjoy my work. But if you enjoy what I create and appreciate real wit, people will think you're wise.

Now I call on the gods to join us in our chorus! Zeus, king of all, god of thunder! Poseidon, shaker of the earth and ruler of the sea! Aether, the life-giving sky! And Sun, who fills the world with light! You shine on gods and humans alike.

Smart audience—listen closely. We, the Clouds, are angry. Even though we help your city more than any other gods, you don't worship us, pour us offerings, or thank us. But we watch over everything. Whenever you make foolish decisions—like voting for that leather-working loudmouth Cleon—we try to warn you. We thunder. We drizzle. We frown.

When you tried to make Cleon your general, we got furious! Lightning struck, the moon skipped her route, and the sun shrank his light in protest. And yet—you still chose him.

You say your city always makes bad choices, but we turn them around for your benefit. And we'll help again—if you punish Cleon for his greed and crimes, and lock him up. Then your city can go back to being strong and proud.

Now hear us again—Phoebus Apollo of Delos, who stands tall on Mount Cynthus! And Artemis of Ephesus, honored by the Lydian girls! Athena, protector of Athens! Dionysus of Delphi, dancing with torches on Parnassus!

When we came here, the Moon stopped us. She told us to greet the Athenians and their allies—but also to complain. She's been treated badly, even though she helps you all the time.

She gives you moonlight so you don't need to buy torches at night. People used to say, "Don't waste money—just walk by moonlight." But now you mix up the calendar, mess up the dates, and the gods don't get their proper offerings. Sometimes, when we're supposed to be fasting in mourning for fallen heroes like Memnon or Sarpedon, you're throwing parties and making toasts.

That's why Hyperbolus, who was chosen as a religious official this year, lost his title. We gods took it away. Let that be a lesson—live according to the Moon's time.

Socrates:

By Air, Chaos, and Breathing—I've never seen anyone so rude, impossible to teach, clueless, and forgetful! He forgets little lessons before he even learns them. Still, I'll drag him out into the light. Where's Strepsiades? Bring out your bed!

Strepsiades (from inside):

The bedbugs won't let me bring it out!

Socrates:

Hurry up and lay it down—and pay attention.

[Strepsiades enters.]

Strepsiades:

Alright, alright.

Socrates:

So, tell me—what would you like to learn first, since you've never been taught anything? Should we start with measuring, or rhythms, or poetry?

Strepsiades:

Measuring sounds good—I just got tricked out of two measures of grain by a food seller.

Socrates:

That's not what I meant. I mean which is a better kind of poetic measure—the trimeter or the tetrameter?

Strepsiades:

Let's bet on it: if a half-pint isn't a tetrameter, I'll be surprised.

Socrates:

Ugh, get lost! You're so uncultured and dense. Maybe you could handle learning rhythms?

Strepsiades:

But what good are rhythms for making a living?

Socrates:

For starters, to sound smart at parties. You'll know what rhythm a war dance follows, or what kind goes with a dactyl.

Strepsiades:

Dactyl? Oh sure, I know that one!

Socrates:

Really? Explain.

Strepsiades:

It's this finger here! When I was a kid, we used to say that!

Socrates:

You're hopeless.

Strepsiades:

Because I don't care about this stuff, you pest! I just want to learn that one argument—that sneaky one.

Socrates:

You can't skip straight to that. First you need to learn about grammar—like which animals are grammatically male.

Strepsiades:

I already know that! Ram, goat, bull, dog, rooster.

Socrates:

See, you're already messing up. You used the same word for both the male and the female rooster.

Strepsiades:

How did I do that? Tell me.

Socrates:

You called them both "rooster." But the female should be "hen," and the male "rooster."

Strepsiades:

Oh, I see! That's great! Just for that, I'll fill your flour jar to the top!

Socrates:

You're doing it again! That jar you mentioned is a feminine word, but you treated it like it's masculine.

Strepsiades:

What? How is that wrong?

Socrates:

Just like if you called a woman "Cleonymus."

Strepsiades:

But Cleonymus didn't have a flour jar—he used to knead dough in a bowl! So what should I call it now?

Socrates:

Call it kardope, like you say Sostrate.

Strepsiades:

So kardope is the right word? In the feminine?

Socrates:

Yes, that's correct.

Strepsiades:

But doesn't that sound like Kleonyme?

Socrates:

You still need to learn which names are masculine and which are feminine.

Strepsiades:

I know the female ones!

Socrates:

Go ahead. List them.

Strepsiades:

Lysilla, Philinna, Clitagora, Demetria.

Socrates:

Now what about the male ones?

Strepsiades:

Tons of them—Philoxenus, Melesias, Amynias.

Socrates:

No, you fool! Those aren't masculine.

Strepsiades:

They're not? But they're men, aren't they?

Socrates:

No way. How would you call out to Amynias if you saw him?

Strepsiades:

Easy. I'd say, "Hey, Amynia! Come here!"

Socrates:

See? You just called him a woman!

Strepsiades:

Well, maybe he deserves it—he never joins the army! But really, why do I have to learn all this stuff that everybody already knows?

Socrates:

It's no use arguing. Now lie down here.

Strepsiades:

What do I have to do now?

Socrates:

Think about your own problems now.

Strepsiades:

Not here, please! Let me lie on the ground if I have to think hard.

Socrates:

Nope. This is the only way.

[Socrates exits.]

Strepsiades:

Poor me! The bugs are going to eat me alive tonight!

Chorus:

Now concentrate and think carefully. Wrap yourself up tight and roll around if you need to. Try new ideas quickly if you get stuck. But don't even think about falling asleep!

Strepsiades:

Ouch! Ouch!

Chorus:

What's wrong? Why are you yelling?

Strepsiades:

These awful bugs are biting me like crazy! They're swarming me, chewing my sides, draining my blood, digging into my guts. I'm done for!

Chorus:

Try not to panic so much.

Strepsiades:

How can I not panic? I've lost my money, my good looks, my life— and even my sandal! And now I'm stuck staying up all night thinking. I'm falling apart.

[Socrates returns.]

Socrates:

Hey you! What are you doing? Aren't you supposed to be thinking?

Strepsiades:

Yes, by Neptune, I am!

Socrates:

Well, have you thought of anything?

Strepsiades:

Just wondering if I'll have any skin left after these bugs are done.

Socrates:

You're hopeless.

Strepsiades:

I feel hopeless, honestly.

Socrates:

Don't give up. Wrap yourself up again. You need to come up with a clever trick to get out of paying debts.

[Socrates paces while Strepsiades rolls in his blanket.]

Strepsiades:

Oh, I wish someone would just throw me a good scam wrapped in a wool coat.

Socrates:

Let's check in on this guy. Hey! Are you sleeping?

Strepsiades:

No, I swear I'm not!

Socrates:

Have you come up with anything?

Strepsiades:

Nothing, except what I'm holding in my hand.

Socrates:

Then focus! Cover yourself up and start thinking.

Strepsiades:

About what, Socrates? Tell me!

Socrates:

You tell me what your goal is first.

Strepsiades:

I've told you a hundred times—I want to avoid paying my debts!

Socrates:

Alright. Then wrap yourself up and take your time thinking through your situation, little by little. Be careful and thoughtful.

Strepsiades:

Oh man, this is rough!

Socrates:

Quiet now. If one idea doesn't work, drop it and try another. Keep your mind flexible.

Strepsiades (excitedly):

Oh, Socrates, my brilliant friend!

Socrates:

What is it?

Strepsiades:

I've got it—a way to dodge the interest!

Socrates:

Let's hear it.

Strepsiades:

Alright, imagine I buy a witch from Thessaly. Then at night, I pull down the moon and trap it in a mirror box, like those helmet cases. I keep it locked up...

Socrates:

And how does that help?

Strepsiades:

Easy! If the moon never rises again, then no one can charge me monthly interest!

Socrates:

Brilliant! Okay, here's another one. Say someone sues you for five talents. How do you get rid of the case?

Strepsiades:

Hmm... let me think...

Socrates:

Stop thinking only of yourself. Let your mind float free, like a beetle tied to a string.

Strepsiades:

Wait! I've got another idea—and it's genius!

Socrates:

Go on.

Strepsiades:

You know those shiny glass stones at the pharmacy? The ones that can start fires?

Socrates:

You mean a magnifying glass?

Strepsiades:

That's it! So I take that, and while the clerk is writing down the lawsuit, I aim it at the sun and burn the letters off the paper from far away!

Socrates:

Amazing! That's clever thinking!

Strepsiades:

Yes! Five talents gone—just like that!

Socrates:

Okay, here's one more. What would you do if you were in court and losing because you didn't have any witnesses?

Strepsiades:

Oh, that's easy.

Socrates:

Let's hear it.

Strepsiades:

I'd leave while another case was being heard, run out, and hang myself!

Socrates:

That's ridiculous.

Strepsiades:

No way! They can't sue me if I'm dead.

Socrates:

You're hopeless. Get out of here—I can't teach you anymore.

Strepsiades:

Why not? Come on, Socrates, please!

Socrates:

You forget everything the moment you learn it. Now tell me—what was the very first thing I taught you?

Strepsiades:

Let me think... what was it again? Oh, what was that thing we use to knead dough? Ugh, I can't remember!

Socrates:

Get lost! You're the most forgetful, most clueless old man I've ever met!

Strepsiades:

Oh no! What's going to happen to me? I'm doomed if I don't learn how to argue properly. Please, Clouds, help me out!

Chorus:

Old man, our advice is this: if you have a grown-up son, send him to study in your place.

Strepsiades:

I do have a strong, good-looking son, but he refuses to learn. What should I do?

Chorus:

Do you just let him disobey you?

Strepsiades:

Yes, he's healthy and strong, and comes from proud city women on his mother's side. But I'll go get him—and if he still refuses, I'll kick him out of the house!

[To Socrates]

Go inside and wait for me just a little while.

[Strepsiades exits]

Chorus:

See how lucky you are to have us on your side? This man will do whatever you ask. So while he's still excited and overwhelmed, make sure you take full advantage of him.

[Socrates exits]

Things like this usually flip around the other way before long.

[Strepsiades returns with his son Phidippides]

Strepsiades:

By Mist, you're not staying in my house anymore! Go live with Megacles and chew on his marble columns!

Phidippides:

Father, what is wrong with you? You're acting totally insane!

Strepsiades:

Listen to that—"Olympian Jupiter!" How silly! You still believe in Jupiter at your age?

Phidippides:

Why do you laugh at that?

Strepsiades:

Because you're still a child inside, holding on to old-fashioned beliefs. Come here—I want to teach you something that'll make you a real man. But don't tell anyone else, okay?

Phidippides:

Fine, what is it?

Strepsiades:

You just swore by Jupiter, right?

Phidippides:

Yes.

Strepsiades:

See how useful learning is? There's no such god as Jupiter!

Phidippides:

Then who rules the sky?

Strepsiades:

Vortex. He kicked Jupiter out and took his place.

Phidippides:

What nonsense is this?

Strepsiades:

I'm telling you the truth.

Phidippides:

And who told you this?

Strepsiades:

Socrates the Melian, and Chaerephon—the guy who figured out how far fleas can jump.

Phidippides:

You've gone completely mad if you believe those lunatics!

Strepsiades:

Speak respectfully! Don't insult brilliant, wise men—men who live simply, don't waste money on shaving or fancy baths. Unlike you, spending my money as if I were already dead. Now go learn from them for my sake.

Phidippides:

And what could I possibly learn from them?

Strepsiades:

Everything worth knowing. You'll discover how clueless you are. Just wait here—I'll be back soon.

[He runs off]

Phidippides:

What am I supposed to do? My dad's lost his mind. Should I take him to court for insanity? Or go find a coffin-maker?

[Strepsiades returns, holding a rooster in one hand and a hen in the other]

Strepsiades:

Look here—what's this?

Phidippides:

A rooster.

Strepsiades:

Good. And what's this?

Phidippides:

A rooster.

Strepsiades:

You called them both the same? That's just silly. Don't do that again. Call this one the hen, and that one the rooster.

Phidippides:

Hen? Did you learn these clever words by going into that weird school with the "Titans"?

Strepsiades:

And plenty of other things too. But I forget everything right after I learn it—probably because I'm getting old.

Phidippides:

Is that also why you lost your cloak?

Strepsiades:

I didn't lose it—I gave it up to focus on learning.

Phidippides:

What about your slippers, you fool?

Strepsiades:

I used them for important needs—just like Pericles did. Now come on, let's go. And if you just listen to me for once, go ahead and mess up later if you want. I remember when you were only six, barely able to talk, and I still bought you a toy cart at the festival with the first coin I earned in court.

Phidippides:

You're going to regret this one day.

Strepsiades:

I'm proud of you for listening to me. Now come on, Socrates! Come out here—I've brought my son, though I had to convince him pretty hard.

[Socrates enters]

Socrates:

He still seems immature. He's not used to our ways yet.

Phidippides:

And you'd be used to hanging—if you ever tried it.

Strepsiades:

Watch your mouth! Don't insult your teacher!

Socrates:

"Hanging"? Did you hear how badly he said that? His mouth was wide open. How's he ever going to win a lawsuit or defend himself in court? And yet Hyperbolus paid a whole talent to learn this stuff.

Strepsiades:

Don't worry, just teach him. He's smart. When he was little, he used to build little houses and ships inside, even made wagons from leather and frogs from pomegranate peels. You wouldn't believe how clever he was! Just make sure he learns those two arguments—the better one (whatever that is), and especially the worse one, which can twist justice to win. If not both, then at least teach him the worse one.

Socrates:

He'll learn them directly—from the arguments themselves.

[Socrates exits. Just and Unjust Causes enter]

Just Cause:

Come here! Show yourself to the people—even though you're shameless.

Unjust Cause:

Go wherever you like. I'll beat you if I speak in front of a crowd.

Just Cause:

Beat me? Who do you think you are?

Unjust Cause:

I'm a cause.

Just Cause:

Yeah—the bad one.

Unjust Cause:

But I'm still better than you. I win.

Just Cause:

By using what sneaky trick?

Unjust Cause:

By inventing new ideas.

Just Cause:

That's just because dumb people support your nonsense.

Unjust Cause:

No—smart people do.

Just Cause:

I'll destroy you.

Unjust Cause:

How?

Just Cause:

By standing up for what's right.

Unjust Cause:

And I'll beat you by challenging everything you say. I say justice doesn't even exist.

Just Cause:

You're denying justice?

Unjust Cause:

Sure. Where is it?

Just Cause:

With the gods.

Unjust Cause:

Then why didn't Zeus get punished for tying up his own father?

Just Cause:

Ugh! That kind of talk is spreading everywhere! I need a bucket—I'm going to be sick!

Unjust Cause:

You're old and ridiculous.

Just Cause:

And you're shameless and disgusting.

Unjust Cause:

Thanks for the compliments!

Just Cause:

You're a brown-noser and a liar.

Unjust Cause:

Wow, you're making me look great.

Just Cause:

And you'd betray your own parents.

Unjust Cause:

You don't realize it, but you're praising me with gold.

Just Cause:

I meant lead, not gold.

Unjust Cause:

Well now it's an honor!

Just Cause:

You're unbelievably rude.

Unjust Cause:

And you're old-fashioned.

Just Cause:

Because of you, none of our young people want to go to school anymore. Someday the Athenians will figure out what kind of nonsense you're teaching these gullible kids.

Unjust Cause:

And you look like a mess.

Just Cause:

And look at you now—so full of yourself. But you used to be a beggar, remember? You claimed to be like Mysian Telephus and wandered around quoting bits of philosophy from a tiny bag.

Unjust Cause:

Oh, how wise—

Just Cause:

Oh, how foolish—

Unjust Cause:

—your insults are!

Just Cause:

And it's a disgrace to our city that they support you, someone who corrupts our young people.

Unjust Cause:

You won't be teaching this boy—old fool.

Just Cause:

Yes, I will, if he wants to become a decent man and not just a smooth talker.

Unjust Cause (to Phidippides):

Come with me. Leave that crazy old man alone.

Just Cause:

Touch him, and I'll make you regret it.

Chorus:

Enough of the shouting! Show us instead what each of you teaches. The old way versus the new way. Then the boy can decide which path to follow.

Just Cause:

Fine with me.

Unjust Cause:

Same here.

Chorus:

Who wants to go first?

Unjust Cause:

He can start. Then I'll use new ideas and arguments to tear his words apart. If he dares whisper anything, I'll sting him all over with sharp points—like a swarm of bees.

Chorus:

Alright. Each of you will try to prove your way is better using clever ideas and strong reasoning. Let's hear what the old-fashioned values really were. Speak up, and show us your nature.

Just Cause:

Here's how things used to be when I was young, and when people still valued discipline and justice. First, boys weren't allowed to speak out of turn. They would walk together to the music school in neat lines, even if it was snowing hard. They had to go barefoot and learn proper songs passed down from our fathers—like "Pallas, destroyer of cities," or other noble tunes.

If someone tried to be funny or added silly twists to the songs like people do now, the teacher would beat them—because that kind of behavior chased the Muses away. In the gym, boys had to sit modestly and cover their thighs, so they didn't show anything improper. When they stood up, they had to smooth the sand to hide their body marks— so admirers couldn't stare.

Boys back then never oiled their bodies below the waist, and they looked healthy and strong. They didn't flirt or change their voices to sound soft and girly. At dinner, it was rude to grab the top of a radish, steal parsley from elders, gobble up fish, laugh too loudly, or sit with legs crossed.

Unjust Cause:

Ugh! That's so old-fashioned—like something out of an ancient festival, all crickets and dusty traditions.

Just Cause:

And yet that strict training created the men who fought bravely at Marathon! Your way, on the other hand, fills today's youth with nonsense. They don't even honor Athena properly at festivals anymore. So, young man, if you choose me, I'll teach you to hate the chaos of the market, avoid fancy baths, be ashamed of bad behavior, get angry when insulted, respect your elders, obey your parents, and live with modesty.

You won't run off to chase dancers or get tricked by girls throwing apples at you. You won't talk back to your father or insult his old age, which helped raise you.

Unjust Cause:

If you listen to that guy, kid, you'll turn into a total loser—like one of Hippocrates' soft sons. Everyone will laugh at you.

Just Cause:

No, you'll live strong and proud. You'll train at the gym, not hang around the market making rude jokes. You won't chase tiny lawsuits or be a greedy trickster. You'll go running through the olive groves of the Academy with other decent youths, crowned in white reeds and breathing in the scents of spring, enjoying the sound of the trees whispering around you.

If you follow my path, you'll have a strong chest, clear skin, broad shoulders, few words, big hips, and little desire for trouble. But if you follow him, you'll be pale, narrow-shouldered, big-mouthed, small-hipped, and full of bad desires. He'll teach you to think bad things are good and good things are bad. And worst of all, he'll fill your mind with disgusting, twisted desires—like that awful poet Antimachus.

Chorus:

Oh you, master of lofty, famous wisdom! Your words have such a calm and graceful power. People in the old days must've been lucky to live when your values ruled. But now, you with your sweet-talking style—it's your turn to speak up and bring something new. He's impressed everyone, so you'll need strong arguments to defeat him or risk becoming a joke.

Unjust Cause:

I've been holding back, but I'm ready now to shake things up with the opposite of everything he said. People call me "the Worse Argument" for a reason—because I was the first to figure out how to argue against the law and justice. And that's worth way more than money! I can take a weak side in a debate and still win. So let's begin with something simple—he said people shouldn't bathe in warm water. But tell me, what's so bad about warm baths?

Just Cause:

Because they make you soft and weak.

Unjust Cause:

Gotcha! Answer this: Which of Zeus's sons do you think was the strongest and bravest?

Just Cause:

No one beats Hercules.

Unjust Cause:

Exactly. And did Hercules ever take cold baths? Nope. Yet he was the toughest of them all!

Just Cause:

That's the kind of thinking that fills bathhouses with lazy kids chattering all day while the gyms sit empty.

Unjust Cause:

You also complain about them hanging out in the marketplace. But I say it's a good thing! If it were bad, why would Homer have shown Nestor and the other wise men spending time there?

Now, let's talk about the tongue. You say kids shouldn't practice speaking. But I say they should. And modesty? Please—that's another big mistake. Show me one person who's gained anything from being modest. Just one!

Just Cause:

Peleus, for example. He was given a sword for his modesty.

Unjust Cause:

A sword? Big deal! Meanwhile, Hyperbolus the lamp-maker got rich through shady deals—and no sword required.

Just Cause:

But Peleus married the goddess Thetis because he was modest.

Unjust Cause:

Yeah, and then she left him. Why? Because he wasn't fun in bed! Women love men who are bold, not shy. You, sir, are completely out of touch.

Now listen, young man. If you follow his ideas, you'll miss out on all the fun—no girls, no games, no tasty food, no parties, no laughs. What's the point of life without those?

And what if you make a mistake, like falling in love or getting caught cheating? With his way, you'll be doomed. But with me, you can enjoy yourself and not feel bad. If someone catches you fooling around, just say, "I didn't do anything wrong!" And remind them that even Zeus falls for women all the time. If a god can't resist love, how can a human?

Just Cause:

But what if he gets punished—like having a radish shoved where it doesn't belong or getting burned with hot ashes? What argument will he use to claim he's not a total creep?

Unjust Cause:

So what if he is a creep? What real harm is there?

Just Cause:

What more harm could there be?

Unjust Cause:

Alright, let's say I beat you in this debate. Then what?

Just Cause:

I'll stay quiet. What else can I do?

Unjust Cause:

Let me ask—where do lawyers come from?

Just Cause:

From the worst kind of people.

Unjust Cause:

True! And what about playwrights?

Just Cause:

Also from the worst kind of people.

Unjust Cause:

And public speakers?

Just Cause:

Same group.

Unjust Cause:

So you admit that all the people society looks up to come from my side. Look at the audience. Which group is bigger—mine or yours?

Just Cause:

Let me see… Oh wow. Yeah, there are way more of your kind—especially that guy with the long hair.

Unjust Cause:

So what now?

Just Cause:

I give up. You win. Take my cloak—I'm switching sides!

[The two Causes leave. Socrates and Strepsiades enter again.]

Socrates:

So, what do you want now? Take your son and leave, or should I keep teaching him?

Strepsiades:

Keep teaching him! And train him well—so he can win small cases and big ones too. Sharpen his tongue so he can argue his way out of anything.

Socrates:

Don't worry. He'll come back a true master of words.

Strepsiades:

More like pale and worn out!

[They leave.]

Chorus:

Go ahead then. But you'll regret this choice.

Now, to the judges—if you help our chorus win fairly, we'll reward you! When you plant your fields in spring, we'll send rain just for you. Others will have to wait. We'll protect your crops from storms and drought. But if you ignore or disrespect us, we'll ruin your harvests. Your vines and olives will get smashed by hail. If you try to make bricks, we'll pour rain and wreck your work. And if you—or someone in your family—tries to get married, we'll rain all night long! You'll wish you were in Egypt instead of here if you judge unfairly!

[Strepsiades re-enters, carrying a sack of flour.]

Strepsiades:

The fifth... the fourth... the third... then comes the second... and after that, the one I fear the most—Old and New Day. That's the day all my lenders threaten me. They say they'll ruin me, they've even filed their complaints already. But all I ever ask is something reasonable— "Sir, please don't collect everything now. Can you delay part of it? Can you forgive a little?" But they just yell that I'm unfair and say they'll sue me.

Well, let them sue me! I don't care anymore, as long as Phidippides has learned how to argue his way out. I'll find out now by knocking on the school door.

(Knocks)

Hey, boy! Anyone there?

(Socrates enters)

Socrates:

Good morning, Strepsiades.

Strepsiades:

Same to you. Please accept this little gift—teachers should be rewarded. Now, tell me, has my son learned that argument you told me about earlier?

Socrates:

He has.

Strepsiades:

Wonderful! Thank you, dear Lady Trickery!

Socrates:

He's now ready to win any case, no matter what.

Strepsiades:

Even if there are witnesses who saw me borrow money?

Socrates:

Yes! Even if a thousand saw it.

Strepsiades:

Then I'll shout this loud: Cry, all you greedy lenders—your money, your interest, and your threats mean nothing now! My son is here, sharp-tongued and ready to defend me. He'll protect my home, crush my enemies, and finally bring peace to my troubled life. Go get him for me, please!

(Socrates exits and returns with Phidippides)

Strepsiades:

Oh my boy! My dear boy!

Socrates:

Here he is. Take him and go.

(Socrates exits)

Strepsiades:

Oh yes! Just look at you! That clever look on your face! You've already got that sharp, arguing expression. You look like someone ready to twist words and play innocent while making others feel guilty. That's the Athenian way! Now, you must help me—since it's your fault I'm in debt, it's your job to get me out of it.

Phidippides:

What are you so worried about?

Strepsiades:

It's the Old and New Day.

Phidippides:

What's that? How can one day be both old and new?

Strepsiades:

That's what they call the day people file lawsuits.

Phidippides:

Well, then they're wrong—two days can't be one.

Strepsiades:

They can't?

Phidippides:

Of course not. That would be like saying the same woman is both old and young at once.

Strepsiades:

But it's the law!

Phidippides:

Then they've misunderstood the law.

Strepsiades:

Then what does the law mean?

Phidippides:

Solon, the lawgiver, supported common people.

Strepsiades:

That doesn't explain Old and New Day!

Phidippides:

Solon set the law so that two days—Old and New—could be used for lawsuits, giving people the chance to settle things early before the new month starts.

Strepsiades:

Why include the "old" day?

Phidippides:

So people could show up a day early and work things out. If they didn't, they'd have to face legal trouble the next day.

Strepsiades:

Then why do the magistrates take deposits on Old and New instead of just the New?

Phidippides:

They act like greedy merchants—jumping at the chance to grab people's money a day sooner.

Strepsiades:

(Happily to the audience) Ha! Did you hear that? You clueless fools! We, the smart ones, are your masters! You're all just empty pots— useless unless we fill you. I should celebrate myself and my brilliant son. Everyone will envy me when he starts winning cases. But first, let me take him inside and treat him to a meal.

(Strepsiades and Phidippides exit)

Pasias (entering with a witness):

Should I just let people keep my money? Never! I'd rather get into trouble than give up my rights. That's why I'm dragging you here, as my witness. I'm even risking making an enemy out of my fellow citizen. But I will never dishonor my country. I'm taking Strepsiades to court.

Strepsiades (from inside):

Who's there?

Pasias:

It's for Old and New Day.

Strepsiades:

Take note, everyone—he said "two" days. So what are you suing me for?

Pasias:

I'm here to collect the twelve minae you borrowed when you bought that gray horse.

Strepsiades:

A horse? Me? You all know I can't stand horses!

Pasias:

But you swore by the gods that you'd pay it back!

Strepsiades:

Sure, back then my son Phidippides hadn't yet learned how to argue so cleverly.

Pasias:

And now you think that excuses you from paying your debt?

Strepsiades:

What else would I gain from sending him to that school?

Pasias:

Are you really going to deny your debt under oath?

Strepsiades:

Oath to what gods?

Pasias:

To Jupiter, Mercury, and Neptune.

Strepsiades:

Sure! I'd even throw in three extra coins to make it official.

Pasias:

You're shameless! May you pay for your tricks someday!

Strepsiades:

You'd be better off getting scrubbed with salt.

Pasias:

You're making fun of me now?

Strepsiades:

He could hold six gallons of nonsense in his head!

Pasias:

By all the gods, you won't get away with this!

Strepsiades:

Your gods make me laugh. Only fools still swear by Jupiter.

Pasias:

You'll regret this. Just tell me—are you going to pay or not?

Strepsiades:

Hold on, I'll give you a clear answer.

(He runs inside the house.)

Pasias (to Witness):

What do you think he's going to do?

Witness:

I think he'll pay you.

(Strepsiades re-enters carrying a kneading trough.)

Strepsiades:

Now, where's the guy asking for his money? Tell me—what's this?

Pasias:

It's a kneading trough.

Strepsiades:

And yet you call it a kardopos? You don't even know the right name for it. Why should I pay anything to someone so clueless?

Pasias:

So you're not paying?

Strepsiades:

Not a coin, as far as I know. Now get away from my door!

Pasias:

Fine! But I swear I'll file a complaint. I'll take this to court!

Strepsiades:

Then you'll lose even more than your twelve minae. Still, I'd hate to see that happen—just because you didn't know the right word.

(Pasias and Witness exit. Amynias enters.)

Amynias:

Oh no, this is terrible!

Strepsiades:

Who's this whining now? Sounds like one of those tragic actors.

Amynias:

Why do you care? I'm just a miserable man.

Strepsiades:

Then carry on being miserable.

Amynias:

Oh cruel fate! The wheels of my chariot broke. Oh Athena, you've ruined me!

Strepsiades:

What did Tlepolemus ever do to you?

Amynias:

Don't joke! Just tell your son to give back the money he borrowed—especially now that I've had such bad luck.

Strepsiades:

What money?

Amynias:

The money he borrowed from me.

Strepsiades:

Then you really were unlucky.

Amynias:

By the gods, I crashed while driving my chariot!

Strepsiades:

You sound like someone who fell off a donkey.

Amynias:

Is it foolish to want my money back?

Strepsiades:

You don't sound right in the head.

Amynias:

Why not?

Strepsiades:

It's like your brain got knocked loose.

Amynias:

By Hermes, if you don't pay me, I'll drag you to court!

Strepsiades:

Answer me this: do you think rain always comes from new water, or does the sun just recycle what's already here?

Amynias:

I don't know, and I don't care!

Strepsiades:

Then why should you get your money back if you don't understand the science behind it?

Amynias:

Fine! At least pay me the interest.

Strepsiades:

What sort of beast is "interest"?

Amynias:

It means the money grows—day by day, month by month.

Strepsiades:

Interesting. So tell me—is the sea any bigger today than it was in the past?

Amynias:

No, of course not. It stays the same size.

Strepsiades:

Then how can your money grow while the sea, into which all rivers flow, stays the same? Now get off my property! Bring me the cattle prod!

(Servant enters with a goad.)

Amynias: I call all of you to witness what's happening!

Strepsiades (hitting him): Go on, get out of here! What are you waiting for? Move along, you horse-lover!

Amynias: Isn't this an insult?

Strepsiades: Move faster!

(He pokes him from behind with a stick.)

I'll keep prodding you, even if I have to poke you all the way to your fancy chariot. Are you running now?

(Amynias runs away.)

I knew that would get you moving—just like your racing horses and wheels!

(Strepsiades leaves.)

Chorus: See what happens when someone loves doing wrong? This old man took that path and now wants to get out of repaying his debts. But something bad is definitely coming his way—maybe even for that so-called teacher of his. I bet he'll regret it when he realizes that his son has become so good at arguing, he can win even with the worst ideas. And Strepsiades might just wish his son couldn't speak at all.

Strepsiades (running out of the house, being chased by his son): Help! Help! Neighbors! Family! Someone stop him! He's beating me! Oh, my poor head and jaw! My own son is hitting me!

Phidippides: Yes, I am.

Strepsiades: Did you hear that? He admits it—he's hitting his father!

Phidippides: I sure am.

Strepsiades: You awful, heartless boy! You're acting like a criminal!

Phidippides: Say even worse things if you want. I actually enjoy hearing insults.

Strepsiades: You're a scoundrel!

Phidippides: Throw some flowers on me while you're at it.

Strepsiades: Are you really beating your own father?

Phidippides: And I can prove that it's fair, too. I'll win the argument.

Strepsiades: You monster! How can it ever be right to hit your own dad?

Phidippides: I'll explain it clearly. You won't be able to argue against it.

Strepsiades: Are you serious?

Phidippides: Completely. Choose which side you want to take: the better argument or the worse one.

Strepsiades: So this is what I paid for you to learn? To argue against what's right?

Phidippides: I'll make you believe it's actually fair to hit a father. Once you hear me out, you'll agree.

Strepsiades: Fine. Let's hear it.

Chorus: It's up to you now, old man. If he didn't think he could win, he wouldn't be so confident. There must be something backing him up. It's obvious he has no shame. So go ahead and tell us what started the fight.

Strepsiades: Okay, I'll explain how it all began. After dinner, I asked him to play a song by Simonides—the one about shearing a ram. But he said that singing and playing the lyre while drinking was old-fashioned, like something a woman grinding flour would do.

Phidippides: Shouldn't I have beaten you right then and there? Asking me to sing like some kind of chirping bug?

Strepsiades: He was already saying crazy things then—just like now. He even said Simonides was a terrible poet. I barely held in my anger, but I stayed calm. Then I asked him to at least put on a wreath and recite something from Aeschylus. But he mocked Aeschylus, saying he was all noise and nonsense, with clunky, awkward language. That really got to me, but I still tried to stay calm. So I asked him to share something from a newer poet if that's what he preferred. Then he recited a part from Euripides about a brother—may bad luck fall on him!—who was involved with his own sister. That was the last straw. I yelled at him with everything I had. And after that, we just kept arguing, one insult after another. Then he jumped on me, started hitting me, choking me, and hurting me.

Phidippides: Didn't I have a good reason to hit you when you don't even respect Euripides, the smartest poet?

Strepsiades: You call him the smartest? What should I call you then? But never mind, you're just going to hit me again.

Phidippides: Yes, and rightfully so!

Strepsiades: Rightfully? You ungrateful brat! Who raised you, knew what you wanted when you were just babbling as a baby? If you said "bryn," I'd give you water. If you asked for "mamman," I'd bring you bread. If you said "caccan," I'd take you outside and hold you until you were done. But now, when I cried out because I needed the bathroom, you choked me instead of helping. You're heartless!

Chorus: I bet everyone's eager to hear how he'll defend this. If he can actually convince people after doing something like that, I wouldn't want to be an old person right now. Your job, kid, is to prove it's fair so people think you're right.

Phidippides: It feels amazing to learn new ideas and ignore old rules! When I only cared about horses, I couldn't even speak clearly. But ever since my dad made me stop riding and focus on deep thinking, I've learned how to argue, reason, and question things. And now, I'll prove it's fair to hit your father.

Strepsiades: Go ahead, ride your horses again! I'd rather pay for a whole team of horses than get beaten like this.

Phidippides: Let me get back to what I was saying before. First, let me ask—did you hit me when I was a kid?

Strepsiades: Of course I did! Because I cared about you.

Phidippides: Then shouldn't I care about you in the same way, by hitting you? If hitting is a form of care, why is it fair for you to hit me but not for me to hit you? I was born free, just like you. You say kids cry when hit, but shouldn't fathers cry too? You'll say the law allows kids to be punished. But old people are like children twice over. So isn't it fair that older folks suffer too, since they should know better?

Strepsiades: There's no law that says a father should be beaten!

Phidippides: Wasn't it just a person like us who made that law before? So why can't I now suggest a new law where sons are allowed to hit their fathers too? We'll forgive past beatings we got before this new law. Look at animals like roosters—they fight their fathers, and they don't even make laws!

Strepsiades: If you're so much like roosters, why don't you eat poop and sleep on a perch too?

Phidippides: That's different. Socrates wouldn't agree with you.

Strepsiades: Please stop hitting me. One day you'll regret it.

Phidippides: Why?

Strepsiades: Because I have a right to punish you. And one day you'll want to punish your son if you have one.

Phidippides: But if I don't have a son, then I went through all this for nothing, and you'll just laugh at me when I die.

Strepsiades: Honestly, friends, I think he has a point. Maybe we do deserve this. It's fair that we get punished when we act unjustly.

Phidippides: Wait, I've got another idea.

Strepsiades: No more! I can't take it!

Phidippides: You might not even be mad about it.

Strepsiades: What do you mean? How could I not be?

Phidippides: I'll hit my mother too, just like I hit you.

Strepsiades: What?! That's even worse!

Phidippides: But what if I win the argument using the worse cause, proving that it's fair to hit my mom?

Strepsiades: If you say that, I'm throwing you and your "worse argument" down a hole with Socrates. This is all your fault, Clouds! You made me trust these people!

Chorus: No, this is your own doing. You chose a dishonest path.

Strepsiades: Why didn't you warn me? You gave me hope and tricked an old farmer.

Chorus: That's what we do to people who love cheating—we let them fall into trouble so they'll learn to respect the gods.

Strepsiades: You're right. I shouldn't have refused to pay back the money I borrowed. Come with me, my son! Let's burn down that lying school and take down Socrates and his friend who tricked both of us!

Phidippides: I won't hurt my teachers.

Strepsiades: Oh come on—respect Father Zeus!

Phidippides: Zeus? You're so outdated. Zeus doesn't rule anymore. Vortex took over.

Strepsiades: Vortex didn't replace him! That's what I thought because of all this nonsense. Oh no… I treated a clay pot like a god!

Phidippides: Talk to yourself, old man.

(Phidippides leaves.)

Strepsiades: I'm going crazy! I must've been out of my mind to throw out the gods for Socrates' nonsense. Oh, Hermes, please don't be mad. Help me. Should I take them to court? Or… no, you're right—I'll burn down their school instead!

Hey, Xanthias! Grab a ladder and a crowbar. Climb up on that roof and tear it down! Do it for me, your master!

(Xanthias climbs up.)

And someone bring me a torch! It's time they paid for what they've done!

1st Disciple (from inside): Hey! What are you doing?

Strepsiades: What am I doing? Just arguing... with your roof beams!

(He lights the roof on fire.)

2nd Disciple: You're going to kill us!

Strepsiades: That's the idea! Unless this roof collapses on me first!

Socrates (inside): What are you doing up there?

Strepsiades: Just walking on air, thinking about the sun—just like you taught me.

Socrates: I'm suffocating! I'm going to die!

Chaerephon: I'm going to burn up!

Strepsiades: That's what you get for mocking the gods and spying on the moon! Go ahead, hit them! Throw things! Do whatever you want—they deserve it for turning against the gods!

(The school burns down.)

Chorus: Let's go. Our work here is done.

The End

Thank You for Reading

Dear Reader,

We hope this timeless classic has sparked your imagination and enriched your literary journey. Now that you've turned the final page, we want to share a vision for the future of reading—one where every classic you've ever wanted to explore is at your fingertips, in a format that best suits your life.

We'd like to invite you to gain immediate, unlimited digital & audiobook access to hundreds of the most treasured literary classics ever written—along with the option to secure deluxe paperback, hardcover & box set editions at printing cost. Together, we can spark a new global literary renaissance alongside our small, independent publishing house called "The Library of Alexandria."

Thousands of years ago, the Library of Alexandria stood as a beacon of knowledge—until it was lost to history. We aim to reignite that spirit of preservation and discovery right now, in the modern age—only this time, it's accessible to all, in every language and every format.

Picture a world where every timeless classic, novel, poem, or philosophical treatise is not only available to read but also updated for today's readers—modernized, translated into any language or dialect, and ready to enjoy in any format you choose, whether that is in an eBook, audiobook, paperback, or deluxe hardcover & box set version a printing cost.

By joining our movement to rebuild the modern Library of Alexandria, you become part of an unprecedented mission to offer:

- **Unlimited Audiobook & eBook Access to the Greatest Classics of All Time**

  Instantly explore thousands of legendary works, from Plato and Shakespeare to Jane Austen and Leo Tolstoy. All are instantly ready to read or listen to, giving you a complete literary universe at your fingertips.

- **Paperback & Deluxe Editions at Printing Costs:**

  Purchase any title in a paperback, deluxe hardbound, or deluxe boxset edition at printing costs, shipped right to your doorstep. Curate your personal library of Alexandria with editions worthy of display—crafted to last, designed to captivate, and delivered straight to your door.

- **Modern translations for Contemporary Readers in all languages and dialects**

  Discover a vast selection of classics reimagined in clear, current language—no more struggling with outdated phrases or obscure references. Next to the original versions, we aim to offer translations in as many languages and dialects as possible.

  As we continue our translation efforts and add new languages, readers everywhere can connect with these works as if they were written today. By bridging linguistic divides, you're contributing to ensuring that these timeless stories become more meaningful, accessible, and inspiring for people across the globe.

- **Your Personal Library of Alexandria:**

  Over the months and years, you'll curate a unique physical archive of classics—each volume a testament to your taste, curiosity, and love of knowledge. It's not just about owning books—it's about curating a cultural legacy you'll cherish and pass down for generations to come.

- **Join a Global Literary Renaissance:**

  Your support fuels an ongoing mission: allowing us to reinvest in offering deluxe print editions (including special boxsets) at their true cost, broaden the range of available formats and translations, and extend the reach of these works to new audiences worldwide. By joining today, you're not just preserving a legacy of masterpieces; you set in motion a powerful wave of literary accessibility.

  We are more than a publisher—we're a movement, and we can't do it alone. Your support lets us scale our mission, preserving and reimagining history's greatest works for tomorrow's readers.

Become a Torchbearer of knowledge.

Thank you for picking up this book and allowing us into your literary journey. As you turn the pages, know that you're part of something larger: a global effort to keep these stories alive, share their wisdom across borders and generations, and spark a true cultural revival for the modern era.

If this resonates with you—please consider taking the next step by visiting:

www.libraryofalexandria.com

With gratitude and a shared love of knowledge,

The Modern Library of Alexandria Team

Visit:

www.libraryofalexandria.com

Or scan the code below: